"Caring for myself is not self-indulgence, it is self-preservation, and that is an act of political warfare."
~ Audre Lorde

Thorn & Bloom Magazine Issue 01
First published by redrosethorns, March 2025
This Edition published by redrosethorns, November 2025
Copyright © 2025 by redrosethorns Ltd. Liability Co. (USA). All rights reserved.
Edited by Kirsty Anne Richards

ISBN: 979-8-9931229-2-2

Published by redrosethorns Ltd. Liability Co. (USA)
Also operating as redrosethorns Ltd. (UK)
www.redrosethorns.com

Thorn & Bloom

Table of Contents

Table of Contents

redrosethorns publishing

redrosethorns journal

Our core publication, *redrosethorns journal*, is dedicated to exploring themes of mental health, self-care, gender and sexuality, and empowerment. Through the literature we publish, we aim not only to raise awareness of these topics but also to educate, inspire, and empower our readers.

As an online journal, redrosethorns features diverse literary works across all genres and styles, released monthly. To ensure accessibility, all pieces are free to read, and our subscribers receive a featured piece each week, fostering ongoing conversations and engagement.

To learn more, visit our website www.redrosethorns.com

redrosethorns magazines

Our publishing journey began with a print literary magazine - *redrosethorns magazine 01: community/connection* - followed by two more editions - *redrosethorns magazine 02: home/belonging* and *redrosethorns magazine 03: rebellion/conformity* - in our annual series. Each issue was centred around a yearly theme, reflecting both the growth of our platform and the essential conversations needed to foster positive mental health.

After three years, we decided to complete the series as a trilogy, allowing us to shift our focus toward expanding other publications and creating more events that bring these themes to life.

Thorn & Bloom

EDITORIAL DIRECTOR

Kirsty Anne Richards

ABOUT THIS MAGAZINE

Thorn & Bloom is a quarterly publication by redrosethorns Ltd. Liability Co., which focuses on the practice of self-care as a from of resilience and liberation.

The literature published herein speak on topics around socialisation, self-awareness, critical thinking, and invites advice on various self-care practices. Bringing to heed the foundation of self-care is to know and honour one's self. And to get to know one's self, we must also learn about the influences that prevent us from living a fulfilling life.

LANGUAGE DISCLAIMER

Our publications offer literature from a diverse community found within our global society. To honour the voices of our authors, we have deliberately kept various English dialects found within each persons work and their respective spellings.

ABOUT REDROSETHORNS

redrosethorns is an educational publication company, which specialises in literature centred around mental health, self-care, gender & sexuality, and empowerment. Founded on feminist principles which believe that through art and literature, we can foster empathy and connection to empower each other to live our authentic selves, while building a society that is accepting of all diversities.

Kirsty Anne Richards is the founder and editorial director of redrosethorns Ltd. Liability Co. With a background in psychology, gender, and sexuality, she is deeply committed to examining the complexities of identity, empowerment, and well-being. Through her work, she strives to create spaces for meaningful dialogue, challenging conventional narratives and encouraging others to cultivate self-worth beyond societal expectations.

An avid reader, Kirsty Anne embraces literature as a vital part of her self-care practice, weaving its lessons into her daily life. She is passionate about the arts and finds joy in travelling, dancing, and writing. She currently lives in London.

Kirsty Anne

EDITORIAL DIRECTOR

There are two fundamental things we need to understand about self-care. One is that to truly take care of our *selves*, our core beings, we must understand what forces - whether internal or external - prevent us from living our authentic truths, and from positive growth. And two, while self-care can include things like exercise and bubble baths, at its core, it's about building our self-worth through intentional, disciplined action. One of the most important ways we do this is by setting and enforcing boundaries. But there are countless ways we can strengthen our sense of self.

Self-care doesn't eliminate insecurities; rather, it helps us to understand what thought patterns keep us stuck, and encourages us to take action. Whether that's spending more time with people who challenge our perspectives or intentionally sitting with our pain to learn what daily habits we need to help us heal and grow.

Over time, I began to realise that these insecurities weren't just personal, they were reinforced by the very structures we live within. The parallels between our societal systems and unhealthy or abusive relationships became undeniable. Both use the same messaging and tactics to keep us insecure and dependent. Think about all the societal norms we follow simply because we've been led to believe that our worth depends on them.

Structures such as wealth, relationship status, gender, sexuality, race, ethnicity, and nationality shape how society values us and what opportunities we have, no matter where we live. It shouldn't be this way, but it is. Now, imagine knowing yourself so deeply that none of these external factors define you. When we recognise our own worth, we become less susceptible to control, whether by individuals or oppressive systems. Just as abusers exploit vulnerabilities to maintain power, so do those who profit from our insecurities and divisions.

Self-care isn't just about making ourselves feel good. True self-care is a radical act. It gives us the strength to break free from limiting beliefs - both personal and societal - uplift others, and create a world that values diversity, kindness, and collective well-being over profit and control. It might seem impossible at first, but once you start living as your authentic self, confident, strong, and free, it no longer feels like an option. It becomes necessary.

In our first edition of *Thorn & Bloom*, we've included pieces that explore the societal structures that hold us back, explore diverse self-care practices, and challenge conventional ways of thinking. Each piece is meant to help you get unstuck by rethinking personal growth, reconnect with yourself, and cultivate real self-worth.

Our goal is for these stories to inspire and empower you. Happy reading!

no machines droning out there today the dogs barking honks in the valley of roofs that leads to uh the harbor...let's bring in our stuffed animals by boat...the animals we sleep with, hug, never hear from, just feel from...

what would encourage them to talk a bath in the wind? a batch of amphetamines? I'd love to hear what meyer has to say...a cuddly manatee I got during my only trip to florida, fort meyers florida...gray, big nosed, the furry fins...meyer's eyes are stitches intent...he's known me for so long through all the long nights...he'd have opinions I think...

love of my afterlife

maybe the other stuffed animals, being in a circle, would cause meyer to speak of what it means to him to spend a lifetime in bed and not in the water, a lifetime of listening to me sputter when I sleep, the cleft stitched mouth of the manatee opening to make sounds...sounds of the mind of yarn in there, sounds of the yearnin for more company than me...surely that...I get bored by me and I have every reason to be interested in me...but the repetitions are much...there's a kind of buirble of the harbor of the business next to the harbor, cars, trucks, cranes...meyer have you ever thought of running away I could ask meyer have you ever been sick and I did not know it meyer have you ever dreamed of the other manatees that I kidnapped you away from during that trip to the gulf green water a heap of manatees...not a scar on meyer...not a bump...not a bruise...

Abel the ant and his cousins

maybe in the summit of the stuffed animals there would be a script writer or a poet or an astronomer that sees galaxies only button eyes can see...the blackest stars...the galaxies stuffed with filler of dust and shaped like giraffes...meyer could be overwhelmed by the company...meyer could freak out and have a fit and threaten to leave my arms for the arms of another...one of those saws that cuts through cement like scissors cut paper is keening...

"Please refuse permission for production of ENDGAME
by Pretoria Theater and all other future propsals
...to present my work in front of segregated audiences."
Samuel Beckett 28.2.72

Glendarina ????

Blinkie the filly

Edith
former
eel

Rousty rabbit

INCLUDED

Wilmad wombat

Threnody the porcupine

Stoic Sam cub

Lars
lizard

meyer almost hums sometimes...near my ear...a sound of skin with love within...love
ultimate filler....needs emptiness to fill...

being stuffed

Two Excerpts from Decimal Point Wonders of the World: Essay as Collage
by Ben Miller

Introduction

These are self-contained excerpts from a book-length hybrid project entitled *Decimal Point Wonders of the World: Essay as Collage.*

Each series segment is hand-crafted without the use of software. Here, a collaboration between the languages of word, color, and shape, creates an evolving dimensionality of analytic expression. Content is drawn from field notes detailing small experiences that awakened consciousness in a big way, countering the numbing technological onslaught of our A.I. era. The visual intensity of each collage asks the reader to slow down and open up to the physicality of reading, as opposed to gliding over the predictability of an automaton essay text tattooing a screen. The on-going project counts as an opportunity to experiment with many expressive tactile materials and the infinite depth of a blank page.

Image on the left:
On Crowded Sleep
2023
mixed-media collage on 90 lb index paper
(photograph, crayon, typewriter ribbon ink,
pens, markers, product packaging cuttings,
cartoon bits...)
8.5" by 11"

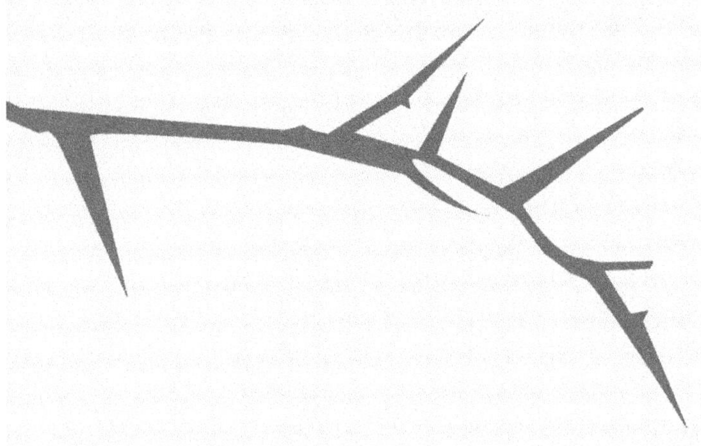

Image on the right:
On the End of Sleep
2023
mixed-media collage on 90 lb index paper (typewriter ribbon ink, pens, marker, highlighter, charcoal, cartoon bits, cut-outs of copy of On Crowded Sleep...)
8.5" by 11"

benny you fell off a fire escape, you cracked your   head opem you bled but the doctor laughe
SEVEN HOURS LATER
a coloring in of a colony
after the fact
beautifulest
Benny, listen to Meyers, you have a way to make it all go away—what pins you down in the dark...a fireman...a fireman placed you gently on the fire escape right at the start, g before the first ounce of night—tucking the blanket, under your chim, wiping your lips
shelves to build a safe
the city—down low, little leap
caught you and no blood no blo
a baby when it counts if
the memory doesn't have
you were caught you were carried
before
every
gory
trap-
parked at the cumb a truck of cribs on fire escapes all over
society out of—babies on fire escapes all over
or roll from safety—and you rolled and the fireman how can you catch
od and no laugh of a drinken sailor— how can you catch a baby, Benny,
you've never practiced catching a baby, Benny, the
to be remembered to be true, does it? and after you
to the truck and placed in the crib with
your Benny name on it, on the metal
shelf in the red cargo bay of the
trucky truck of addresses, babbling
voices of the other brave fire escape
tester volunteers—nothing a baby won't try
once, that's the beautifulest aspect of
babies— drill over, payment in the
form of a yarn helmit of virtue,
with every twist,
on, your uldimate
saved and saved
and saved again
sailors were on
a ship at sea,
far away from
every haven
us is all a matter of guessing
without the crayon of memory
fill of pale wiggling equipment
a christening
bay,
babies— drill
form of a yarn
I hat tippling
sun saying on,
duty is to be
and saved
the drinken
tear it up,
crubs of
11:
WAKE, BENNY;
WAKE — IT'S TIME
TO SWIM-TIME
FOR THE DIVE OFF
THE PI-SALT WILL
SUCK OUT ALL
SPLINTERS
to make a you of I and us
before you tried happlessly told you of you I by or
the wisps of heresay—things
calling you a drunken sailor
unfold a fate, or remold in a way irradiable—true buf mythic also, given us grasping
what happened by us to two to
I lattened my handon the glass of the grass like we were the murse of the ear

Renewal
by Jeremy Gadd

There are so many seeking unicorns,
searching for antidotes to personal poisons,
antivenoms for being treated with scorn
and disdain; medical, financial, emotional
procaine to deal with past or present pain.
Some shellfish coat nacre over irritants
but, similar to cicadas shedding their shells,
deciduous trees their desiccated leaves,
crayfish and crabs their carapace
or human bones, which replace
themselves every decade and enable
physical growth - so compassion and kindness
become balm for sores, ointments to
restore the dismayed and betrayed.

The Lost Art of Writing Letters
by Diana Raab

Before the advent of the Internet we used to write old-fashioned letters to one another that we stamped and mailed. Those of us who remember might have gotten creative and sealed the letter with special sealing wax or maybe a sticker on the back of the envelope. In a sense, with the emergence of email correspondence, letter writing has taken another form, but there's no doubt that there's still something magical about writing and receiving a handwritten letter.

Handwritten Letters

There are many advantages to a handwritten letter, as doing so can be a vital tool for clarifying your feelings to yourself or others. The real purpose of a letter is to inform, instruct, entertain, amuse, explore psychological problems, keep in touch, or even provide something as basic as loving sentiments.

Letters can also be a way to write down thoughts as a segue to face-to-face discussions. Some people use letter writing to release pent-up emotions, such as complaints to companies about malfunctioning products or letters to the editor commenting on current events. Typically, when addressing a particular issue in a letter, it's easier (and healthier) to blow up on the page rather than doing so directly toward an individual. On the other end of the spectrum, it's also amusing to write love letters as a way to express one's innermost feelings.

Many writers are quite good at letter writing. Some use the form of a letter to warm up or get into the swing of their writing practice. It's also a good way to develop one's voice. And, many writers such as myself jot down thoughts in a journal in letter form as a way to get the words flowing. Author John McPhee once said that every book he wrote began with the words "Dear Mother." His letters didn't typically end up in

"How you treat yourself is how you're inviting the world to treat you."
~ Jane Travis

his published books, but they helped him open up to the thoughts and feelings that were currently on his mind.

Another example is diarist Anaïs Nin who began her first journal entry as a letter to her deranged father as a way to remain connected with him. She never actually sent the letter, but it ended up being the spark for her passion for journaling. The truth is, it's not always necessary to mail the letters you write. Sometimes the simple exercise of writing the letter is all that's needed to clear our minds and calm our psyches.

Some people choose to write letters to their pets, but in truth, you can really write to whomever or whatever inspires you. It is important to date your letters, though, so you can keep track of what you were thinking at a particular time. You might even consider making a copy for your records. Sometimes it's amusing and informative to reread letters you've written and sent, and if you're a writer, maybe the contents can be used in a future literary work.

The best way to start a letter is to jot down what prompted you to write in the first place and explain why you were thinking of the recipient at that particular time. The letters we most enjoy receiving are those that reveal the writer's personality. When reading well-written letters, we feel as if the sender is sitting with us, looking us in the eye and speaking to us.

Perhaps the most satisfying aspect of letter writing is the opportunity to communicate exactly what's on your mind. What more could a writer ask for than a specific, hand-picked, captivated reader? So, if you could say anything you wanted to anyone in the world, who would you address? What would you say? Think about it, then sit down, take out a sheet of paper or crack open your journal, choose your audience, and embark on your journey!

Tips for Writing a Letter

•Use simple, easy-to-understand sentences.

•Avoid using long, complicated words.
•Be specific.

•Break your letter into small sections or paragraphs.

•Make sure your voice or tone is appropriate for the subject of the letter.

•For clarity, read the letter aloud.

•Write, rewrite, and polish your letter.

Happy writing!

***

The Accordionist
by Charly Murmann

It was early July, and I was listening to the many songs of different kinds of birds. I was twenty-three years old. I was walking in Plainpalais in Geneva, near the Centre d'art Contemporain and MAMCO, in Switzerland. I was walking hand in hand with my boyfriend. My boyfriend, number three in my third monogamous relationship.

Slowly, I got distracted by the music playing at the end of the oval space where the Flo market was taking place. Number Three went to a kiosk to buy sweets. I told him: I am going to listen to the musician. The accordionist played one of my favourite songs from one of my favourite French films: "Amelie", by Pierre Jeunet. A film that I appreciated for the magic and the gentle kindness of human interactions, which added to the awkwardness of the main characters. I loved the matching colours of red and green in the whole scenography. The objects came alive and became funny creatures to interact with Amelie when she felt lonely.

I saw you from afar, and you smiled at me. You knew what you were doing. I regretted wearing this semi-transparent black and blue flowered dress in two layers that moved up my legs too often. I felt uncomfortable, but it was such a warm day. The sun flirted with the tights attached to my body. I performed the girl. I performed the girl in the dress. Performing straightness. The girl and the boy are read as straight. The girl and the boy walked but did not look in the same direction. The closer my body moved to yours, the more excitement warmed my chest. It was a relief to

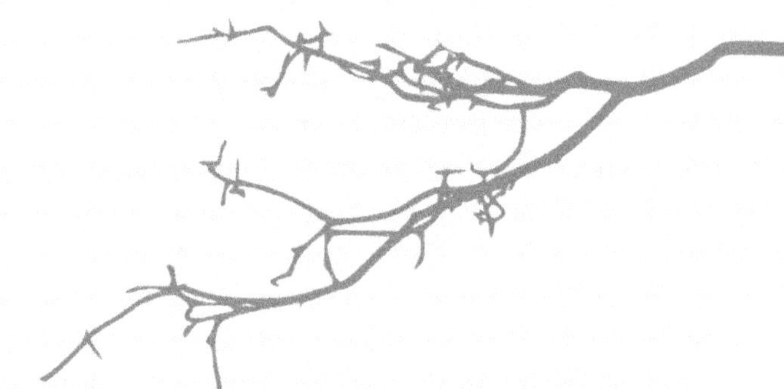

know that Number Three left my hand to grab sugar. I took a few coins from my pocket and placed them in your knitted beige and brightly coloured hat. You smiled at me as bright and big as the toothpaste ad, but at the same time, your green eyes pierced mine. Your red hair and green eyes matched my favourite movie. I wish I wore at least one of those two colours. I wondered if I would be able to exchange words with you. My heart stopped beating. I remembered to breathe. It was one of my first memories of a stranger affecting me so much. You stopped playing and started a conversation with me. You were amazing. I was frozen. I just kept smiling. I try to remember how other people interact with other people. You told me about a feminist event in Geneva next Wednesday. I replied that I would like to come. You told me you lived in Paris. You were only here for a few weeks, on holiday. When Number Three came back and took my hand in his, I left his hand down. I smiled at you. You, the accordionist, replied, "See you soon". Number Three said: Wow, she was flirting with you... I said: No, we were talking about a feminist event next week, I might go, I'll see. He replied: You should go, sounds good.

My body and mind were so drawn to her. I felt like a magnet on a refrigerator, impossible to separate from her image. I was too scared to leave. I was too afraid to feel more. I was too scared to be rejected. I was too afraid to let myself down. I wanted to be brave and just live the experience in the present and see her again. I didn't want to cheat. I hoped to see her again. To see her again in Geneva, hopefully soon. I find excuses not to face my attraction to The Accordionist. I hope that this burning sensation in my chest, my stomach and between my legs will suddenly fade.

I will regret not meeting her on Wednesday. I will regret it for years to come. I will promise myself and my friend Marie that if I see her again, anywhere on the planet, I will kiss her. I thought of her every time I went to bloody Paris.

When I am too shy and not brave enough to flirt with someone, I think of her. I think of her to encourage me to take risks instead of regrets. To take the risk of having my heart broken into pieces and not finding superglue to fix it. To give me the chance to experience queer feelings and connections. To not regret my own desire to feel a spark with someone new. To remember that my heart is not dead. To remember that without trying, nothing will happen. Without trying to build trust, connections don't magically happen. People are meant to communicate through language and bodies. To meet people and create something not through them but with them and grow. How the energies of plants and trees support each other to flourish and take over the world.

Unfortunately, since that anecdote, I have not always been brave and have been quite flaky a few times. But I did tell some people how charming they were. I made compliments about artistic drawings on strangers' tote bags. I've given or exchanged my number at parties. I tried awkward conversations or asked people out. I flirted at queer parties, banks, bookshops, restaurants, universities, art schools, coffee shops, comic festivals, music festivals and my workplaces. At the top of the list: in the queue for the toilet at the open-air cinema and at a cheap student music festival where I was too drunk. I thought saving time and energy was the point, so why not flirt while waiting to pee?

I want to create a space where my emotions can take over my rationalities. I want to create a home where I'm not afraid to fall in love again and again without making fun of myself for trying again and again. I want to be proud that I can give myself a chance to play the game, to nurture connections or walk away if it's not reciprocal. I want a path for myself where I can check in with myself and still be able to build trust with others. To explore connections between souls and to create without categories, names or patterns but with enthusiasm and surprise.

I am crossing my fingers and touching wood to be more present for myself, for others, for the people in between, and for the people I grow with or alongside.

***

Daily Activities
by Joseph Reich

They said that the infamous author Henry Miller
at the end of his life suffered from severe bouts
of nightmares as if even after getting through
all that struggle and suffering and becoming
something of a success his past literally
came back to haunt him while appears
like the human mind deep down inside
just will never let up and never ever

quite get over all that loneliness as in
this case could never really proverbially
escape New York like those little slight
cracks still in the sidewalk and weeds
managing to push their way through.

An interesting phenomenon when my wife
first got pregnant with our child was how
I started dreaming all over again and hadn't
done so for ages just busy trying to survive
and get by in life and when I all of a sudden
started having these very clear and lucid
dreams of my bittersweet childhood...

So maybe it might just be recommended
to take after that old timer who still goes
into work each and every day in that blue
blazer still going through the motions standing
with his age-old briefcase on the edge of the
platform now only working a couple hours
a day at that stock firm or advertising agency

All the clean-cut young bucks kidding around
with him making fun of what's in that briefcase
and him loving it with those silent humble
expressions washing over his face feeling
that sense of belonging and being a part
of things and that supposed team or family
heading back home early to *Grand Central*

still clean and empty before all the craziness
of rush hour as well as the silent surreal local
when he takes that zooming train back to
the suburbs — may even have some

time to help out his lovely wife in the
garden who always stood by his side
still experiencing the keen palpable
sensation of the change of seasons
and trains rattling and whooshing
like the wind in the distance...

Those majestic maples maintenance keeps
in such good shape with those gigantic
regenerating leaves you can rely on
to come out year after year to provide
those sheltering shadows which might escort him
back to where he originally came from and all started.

A Conversation with
Shikha S. Lamba
interviewed by Kirsty Anne Richards

Shikha S. Lamba is a jewelry designer and poet living in Hong Kong. She is the co-editor of an online magazine, *Coffee and Conversations*. Shikha has contributed poetry and visual art for publications in Hong Kong, US, UK, Bangladesh, Indonesia, the Netherlands and India. Her poems and photographs were nominated for Best of the Net in 2023 and 2024. She is a 2023 Pushcart Prize nominee. Passionate about raising awareness about women's health and mental health issues through her writing, her poems often touch on themes of feminism and social injustice. She admittedly lives a big portion of her life online and can be found on most social media sites for her writing, jewelry and magazine.

Kirsty Anne Richards: How did you get started in jewellery design? And what inspires your creations?

Shikha S. Lamba: Jewellery design definitely wasn't my first career choice. In fact, it was not on my radar at all. I wanted to be a journalist or study English Literature, but I did not have the grades required for the college courses I needed to take. I've always been very creative, and was an art student, and one of my aunts recommended jewellery design. I think the design part appealed to me a lot because I don't really wear a lot of jewellery myself. The fashion world does not interest me all that much; I do not have one fashionable bone in my body, but I love creativity.

I am inspired by the variety of gemstones our earth produces, as well as cultural elements from around the world. I see jewellery as a keeper of memories and stories. You wear these pieces during your lifetime, and then you pass them on to future generations, allowing them to accumulate even more stories over the years. To be more environmentally responsible, I specifically use only metals and materials that are durable and can be worked on or redesigned. I love the design aspect of it, the business aspect, not as much.

K: No one likes the business aspect. Do you incorporate cultural influences or meaningful symbols into your jewellery?

S: Yes, a lot. Most of my jewellery is handcrafted and highlights Indian craftsmanship. I use a lot of Indian designs and techniques. The designs start in my mind, then go on to paper, and then in the hands of my karigars (craftsmen) in Delhi and Jaipur. I've lived in Hong Kong for 18-plus years, and I also enjoy using Chinese motifs and gemstones. I love making eclectic pieces that combine elements from different cultures. Those pieces are some of my favourites to design.

K: And then you said you wanted to be a journalist. Is that how you started *Coffee and Conversations*? How did you get into that?

S: I went back to writing poetry after almost a 17-year hiatus in 2018, and during that time, I used to submit my work to *Beyond the Boundaries*, a physical and online magazine in Hong Kong that churned out five issues yearly. Due to some unexpected circumstances, the opportunity to become editor for the magazine came up, so I took up the challenge and delved into a field in which I had zero experience. I loved the job, but I left shortly after a year because the magazine grew significantly that year, and I required a team, which unfortunately couldn't be put into place. Around the same time, my current co-editor and co-founder of *Coffee and Conversations Magazine*, Rashmi, who, I guess, had seen this growth trajectory with *Beyond the Boundaries* over the year, suggested, "Why don't we start our own online magazine?" I said okay, and left a paid gig to start my own magazine.

K: Oh, nice! And what kind of work does *Coffee and Conversations* mainly publish?

S: We publish a variety of content. We have a wellness section for health and wellness articles and a lifestyle section that covers art, travel, photography etc. Under 'Conversations', we publish essays and op-eds, and inspiring stories about people and organizations. Also stories that

"I want to create a space
where my emotions can take
over my rationalities. I want
to create a home where I'm not
afraid to fall in love again
and again without making fun
of myself for trying again
and again." ~ Charly Murmann

are fun and entertaining to read. My favourite might be our Reading Nook, where we cover authors, publish book reviews and poetry.

K: And you said you live in Hong Kong. Is that where the majority of your readership is, in Hong Kong?

S: The majority of our readership is in India, then the US. After that comes Hong Kong and Southeast Asia, and then Europe.

K: That's amazing. And what inspires you to keep the magazine going?

S: I believe one of the reasons I am passionate about my work is because of my love for creativity. I admire it and am even envious of it. If I could, I would do all the creative stuff that's possible, but I do not have the skills or the time for everything. I like providing a platform for deserving work, although the term "deserving" is quite subjective, as it reflects my personal preferences. Nevertheless, I think it's important to highlight people's work because that opportunity is often lacking in many places. Many magazines, such as *Vogue, Variety,* and *Style* etc., focus heavily on fashion and consumerism—topics that have their place but don't necessarily offer substantial reading material. These magazines are often quickly discarded. I stopped buying them a long time ago.

When I came on as the editor of *Beyond the Boundaries*, I was amazed at how much the readership grew in just a year. We didn't really have a 'reading magazine' in Hong Kong, and I wanted to fill that gap. My decision to take that risk paid off; people began to hold onto issues because they enjoyed specific articles or wanted to revisit certain stories.

A lot of the other smaller publications here are heavily driven by advertisements. It's all about what to buy "this season" and what to do this season.

These magazines operate under a capitalist mindset, while I aimed to create a storytelling magazine.

With *Coffee and Conversations,* we have adhered to that vision. While those other platforms serve their purpose, but I'm a bit tired of what they publish. I don't necessarily want to know what else to buy unless, maybe, it's about books.

K: I'm just overwhelmed and exhausted now with advertisements, and I think more and more people are feeling the same way. I see those comments all the time. It's just over and over and over again. And I really wanted to do something, I wanted art. I want people's voices, and I want their stories, and I want their art, their creativity explored and looked at, because...I'm the same as you, I like that, too. I would rather buy a magazine that I can read and keep, something that you can reference back, something that you can enjoy forever, something that you can also pass on. You can't pass on a *Cosmopolitan*, you know, it's dead. It's last year.

S: I just feel most of these magazines don't have the right influence on people either. Looking at the kind of world we're living in, that's not what's going to bring people together or make this world any better. It's not what will foster empathy or connect individuals across cultures. I see that it has its place, but please stop telling us what's "hot" this season, what colour is in etc. Every colour is suitable in every season. Don't tell me pink can't be worn this fall. A lot of this content fills our heads with unnecessary nonsense because instead of thinking about something sensible people are festering over which colours they can't wear. When we're consuming so much rubbish (I'm ready for all the hate mail this is going to bring my way)…then what else are our brains going to fill up with? What else will our conversations be about?

K: Exactly! So much brain rot information when we could be using our time and energy to create more, and foster community instead of sowing division. So, we've already touched on that you are a poet that you started writing 6, 7 years ago…

S: I wrote poetry in school and college. After college I didn't write for a very long time, and started again in 2018-2019.

K: And what inspired you to start writing?

S: I'm not quite sure why, but since I was very young, I've enjoyed playing around with poetry. I appreciate how a story can be conveyed in this format; it's amazing how you can distil an entire world, along with experiences and emotions, into a small poem. I love the depth that poetry offers, allowing so much to be expressed in just a few words. For instance, you can convey a wide range of emotions in a 900-word essay, but doing the same in a ten-line poem feels almost magical.

K: And how does your personal background influence your work? And how does it influence your writing?

S: I think a lot of my writing reflects my Indian culture. I write about my upbringing and my family a lot. Many poems reflect my struggles with my health. Unfortunately a lot of news coming out of India also influences my poetry, especially the patriarchy, rape culture and violence against women etc.

K: Are there any reoccurring themes in your poetry that you particularly feel connected to?

S: I'm connected to almost every piece I write. Some reoccurring themes are about issues I am passionate about, like patriarchy, women's rights, motherhood, etc. I often write about the frustrations and anger I feel regarding the state of the world. Things, people, and places I am inspired by also influence my work. Some poems get to me more than others. Now, perhaps because of my age and hormones, I find myself crying a bit more reading some of my older poems, and I think, Damn! This never made me cry when I was writing it.

…cont. on page 39

Self-care
/self-kare/ noun

The active process of making your body and mind a pleasant place to inhabit, by filling your own cup first. This ensures you have enough to give others.

Two Stories
by Joanne Esser

There are two true stories
of everyone's life.

There's the one you are told
when the person you once loved
slams the door,
pulls out of the driveway
for the last time

and you hear: it's all
your fault. It's always
your fault. If you
 were a better person,
 this would not have happened.

It echoes in your head
like truth, like a priest
or a parent or teacher
 has seen the stains
 in your soul and
 how ugly they are.

You hear it again
 as you're rushing to work,
at the grocery store,
at your child's day care center,
the only story you have time
to listen to.

And then, months later,
or maybe years,
or maybe after you've lived long enough,
the other one:

the one the river whispers
as it flows over rock
smoothing, smoothing,
as it carries winged maple seeds
that have fallen in,
and newly hatched tadpoles
just flexing their tails.

The story of the world in motion.
How nothing is stationary
and all the edges change shape
over time.

To my hands the water offers the story
of rounded stones.

Upon a Slender Stalk
by Deborah Blenkhorn

White coral bells upon a slender stalk,
Lilies of the valley deck my garden walk.
Oh, don't you wish that you could hear them ring?
That can happen only when the fairies sing.
[White Coral Bells nursery rhyme]

Why do I have such a hard time ignoring everyone? It's like a physical ache, this thirtysomething longing to remain where I am, this need to avoid or reject all offers to leave. All I wanted this weekend was to stay home, in my own space: I didn't even answer my phone most times it rang, knowing it was a friend wondering if I wanted to go to church with her on Sunday. That little twinge of guilt is a drop of water in a lake of relief.

This was my goal, my only resolution on hitting my mid-thirties: that I would seize power in a bloody coup, that I would stop feeling manipulated, that I would take charge of my life, that I would stop saying that unconditional yes. But this lesson has been long in the learning, bound up in my memory of the woman who first told me, "You don't have to say yes."

Charlie, wife of my mother's former lover, Stewart, friend of my youth, fellow denizen of the Farm, is very ill right now—has been for a while, but I'm so far away (thousands of miles plus a couple of decades) ... I've just heard about how serious it is in a letter from Stewart. He still maintains their sheep farm and organic garden, although Charlie's health

keeps her off the Island most of the time, close to the constant medical attention she requires. What's wrong? you may ask, and I guess no one knows for sure; that's a major part of the problem. Possibly arsenic or mercury poisoning—sounds quite horrifying. The perils of modern life: from playing golf or getting your teeth filled (hardly to be described as the sins of one's youth), you could have signed up for gut-paralysing pain; you could end up having to get all your nourishment through a feeding tube, all because some nasty substance snuck its way into your blood and your body systems, like the Grinch sneaking into Who-ville on Christmas Eve.

I picture you, Charlie, and I can't add any years to the age you were when I knew you best (more or less my current age, so you see I have caught up to you, my dear): I was a pre-teen; you seemed timeless then, as perhaps you are now. A shock of auburn hair atop a face as fresh and warm and vibrant as any I've seen; laughing blue eyes sparkling with lively good humour and intelligence; a slim, almost boyish, athletic figure ready to dive into one of Canada's Great Lakes, or any adventure, with gusto.

I'm on a winding trip down memory lane. It's a country lane, bordered by Queen Anne's Lace as tall as we are, tall grasses waving gently in a warm breeze. A solid white farmhouse, the Frameworks, stands protectively in the background, ready to shelter us from all the elements, as indeed it does: snow in winter, heat in summer. It's just a short walk to where we're going. The gravel crunches beneath our feet, which are a little too warmly clad in rubber boots on this halcyon day. The sheep in the neighbouring pasture stare at us balefully or turn away, distracted by some choice morsel of grass. Woolly denizens of the fields, they amble unless startled. They are not startled by us, for we meander languidly in the summer heat, as in a

dream. A twinge of sadness, a reassuring squeeze of your hand: that comfort is there as surely as the soft waves of Lake Ontario beside us—we will swim later when our work in the garden is done. We will dive into that lake together, naked as the day we were born, free from farm work for the afternoon, away from the cloying smells of the barn and the sheep.

Even — perhaps especially — on a sheep farm in rural Ontario, there are places of cultivated flora to set your heart singing. Down this path, past the sheep, is an awkward, bespectacled teenage girl, gazing with frank admiration at her gardening companion. I am that girl; the companion is my friend Charlie—and it's a wonderful world that has such creatures in it. You cannot quite explain the connection between woman and girl: a woman, as yet, with no children of her own; and a girl, as yet, unsure of her place in the world. I'll try the word "mentor." I think it fits.

What she gave me — a stronger sense of the world around me and my place in it—was as intangible then as it is now. I recall the minute details of the setting in which we co-existed for a time, and I confess that, for the most part, they elude me. I supply them here in partial semblance of what was real. Even as I conjure up a portrait of this woman who was so central to my life at one time, I cannot make out the colour of her eyes, nor the shape of her smile. But her voice still rings in my ears.

She is teaching me a song, "White Coral Bells," a traditional poem set to music. How many generations of girls and women have sung this song as they planted their gardens? We are probably planting something as unromantic as field tomatoes —or maybe we are actually planting some flowers today—and our attempts to sing the song are punctuated by Charlie's account of her recent run-in with a "renegade" chicken—but the mundane nature of our task notwithstanding, we persevere. The song

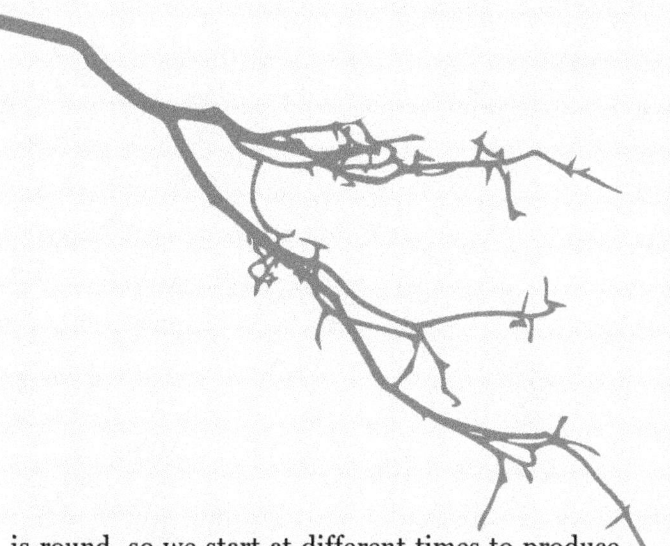

is round, so we start at different times to produce the desired effect of harmony.

When I hear my voice blending so sweetly with hers, I see myself as beautiful, indeed, I know, suddenly, that I am beautiful in her eyes: not some gawky nerd-brain, but a graceful young woman on the threshold of who knows what wonders the world might have in store for me. I know she cares for me, even worries about me, is there for me. I can think of nothing I have done to deserve such care. I am honoured by her trust in me, as we plan to swim together in the lake on the day she goes into labour. Did we actually do so, or just plan it? I imagined it so many times, I cannot tell you. As we sing together today and countless other summer days, I am changed, I am transformed by this friendship with someone so high above me in life and in love.

Charlie: my mother's friend, and then my mother's former lover's lover (as far as I could tell, that was the way things worked on the Farm, the sheep-raising commune of which my mother, my grandmother, and I were sometimes residents); originally I think she and my mother were colleagues during a teaching stint at Seneca College in the Toronto area. When I first met Charlie, she was going out with a huge man who seemed easily twice her size; she told my mother and me an amusing story of sharing — or trying to

share—a small tent with him. To make a long story short (just as well since I don't know the details), she broke up with the big guy, sold the tent, and came to live on the Island with the rest of us.

All times of transplantation are times of loss, but Charlie's laughing eyes concealed whatever tears there may have been. It's mostly times of unremitting joy I remember with her, like the day of her wedding. Oh, how we danced on the day she was wed, Clapton's still-innocent voice proclaiming on the stereo: "I've been waiting so long/ to be where I'm going/ in the sunshine of your love…"

My memories of her keep looping back to her wedding day: how can I describe her, except through the eyes of a fourteen-year-old acolyte? Petals fell from the trees, showering her with their delicate white beauty and fragrance; loving friends gathered to wish her well; she was a fairy princess of delight. She wore a short dress of a pale, light fabric—anything more would have weighed down that spirited sprite. Ethereal, she was connected to everyone and no one. I knew then I could not hold her, that other forces laid claim.

During the time we shared together, she was kept from me by illness only once, confined to her bed with what was perhaps a precursor of her current troubles. Friends were staying with her at the Farm, a couple of women who espoused some alternative medicine philosophy; they monitored her organic diet scrupulously and denied me (who could blame them? but I did) access to her sick room. So, I did not see her suffer at that or any other time that I can recall. Or, more likely, I never really understood her pain, absorbed in myself as the young are wont to be—as I still am in so many ways, having run away from my lessons before learning them fully.

The lesson I failed to learn, "You don't have to say yes," was one that could have saved me from

myself, the self I came to know and despise on an ill-fated student exchange trip to Australia. When I found out I'd been selected to participate in the program, everyone said, "That's great! What an opportunity!" Everyone except Charlie. As we knelt in the garden one day, tending to the last tasks of summer, she looked at me earnestly—and for once, there was no smile illuminating her features. I can still hear her voice, as clear as a bell:

"You don't have to go, you know. You don't have to say yes."

Ah, what wisdom did I lack, that I dismissed her words without really considering them? What arrogance had crept into my soul, that I brushed away the words of my mentor as if they were drops of water blown carelessly from lake or sky?

"Oh no, I want to do it," the words I have repeated so often since, always with a vague feeling of foreboding as I put flesh on the bones of my lie: this body of self-generated conviction will take on a life of its own; I will convince myself. Put those questions aside (what matters if those questions are the fairy dust that can save me from evil? What matters if those questions are the truth, and the answer is a lie?)

Hindsight: then, those years ago, it was so wrong to leave the security I had just found, the sense of self, the sense of family—all so recently acquired, still in fledgling form, so delicate, so new. It was as if I had built myself up to a position of strength, after a long illness in childhood (I speak now of a spiritual dearth) to a position of strength and wholeness and wellness. It was not yet time to try that strength in the wide world; as a patient convalesces in a sunny room before venturing into the bold vagaries of nature, as a lamb born in distress needs special care before it can join the others in the pasture, a vulnerable soul needs time and healing before setting out on an adventure. Charlie knew this, whether from her own experience or from her intuitive connection to the hearts and minds of others; I'm sure she knows it even now.

A year alone in Australia was not, as I painfully discovered, desirable for me—it was not even possible for me, as was clearly apparent when I returned in disgrace to Canada three weeks later. And in those three weeks, I did some damage to myself, such that I was unable to return to the shelter of the love I had left behind. Sometimes, we can hardly face the one who has told us the profound truth to which we did not listen.

Now, I think of what else I learned and am still learning.

I learned how to love, as I now love my friend and current mentor, Emily: Charlie taught me this when I was fourteen. When Charlie gave the official toast to my mother and grandmother at my wedding, almost a decade later, I understood that these women—whom I had by times undervalued in my own life—had been friends and mentors to her in adult life. And if I didn't learn to say no, maybe it was because she was always giving so much of herself that she was ultimately a poor example of denial. And did she find out (did Stewart tell her himself?) that her husband approached a young girl under his guardianship (me) in a way that violated the trust and responsibility reposed in him? Was that the psychological root of her mysterious physical illness?

Now, much louder than the church bells that have failed to summon me this afternoon, those coral bells are pealing.

Oh, don't you wish
That you could hear them ring?
That can happen only when
The fairies sing.

If you hear them, my sweet sprite, may they nourish your body and soul: I wish you well again, with all the fairy magic I can summon.

***

Invisible Stitch
by Kiyoshi Hirawa

Ask if your administration is handling misconduct. Sexual misconduct. And then they'll ask for your badge and gun. And equipment. Then you'll turn in shirts and pants, inadvertent career portfolios sporting dark stains of bodily fluids. Some yours, most not. Vomit from where you dragged someone out of a garage hazy with carbon monoxide. They lived. Blood from a car v. train collision. They died, all of them. Baby spit-up from doing CPR on a three-month-old. Two-finger chest compressions in the back of a wailing, swaying ambulance, paramedics clutching an IV, frantically tapping for a vein. She lived. Her twin did not. But never mind, hand in your jacket. The hat, too, with the badge so shiny you turned it backwards when searching buildings on burglar alarms. They shoot at what's bright. Burglars do, too. Marvel at how items you did not own—not really, they're department-issued—can own your identity, ever more malignant and splintering. Disowned and yet still owned. So turn in your uniform after responding to one thousand seven hundred and four calls for service last year. And all you'll think about are tailors and obstetricians. Because when you heft for the last time that leather snake of a gun belt and bulletproof vest that never contoured to a woman's body, all you see are stitches. Tiny ants secretly scrambling up and down trousers and shirts and jackets, even those clenching the gun belt. Ripping open a scandal for the world—buttons snapping and spraying—will always invite needles. *You don't own these stories*, you told them. *We own your voice*, they told you. And when you own a voice, you may stitch as you please. Until it's comfortable again. Turn in your holster, stitches there, too, among the plastic, and recall your first perineal stitch after your second child. Your discomfort accommodating someone else's comfort. What's owned can always be sewn. The maddening paradox of disownment. Return what's yours, yet what you don't own. So you can be owned, then sewn, invisible stitches crisscrossing the length of your body from lips to lips.

- for all victims of police sexual violence, including women police officers

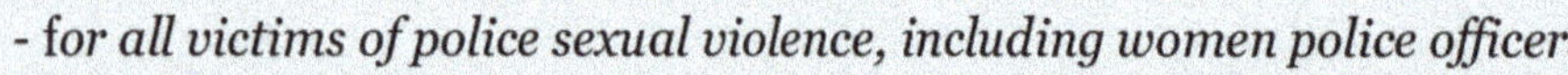

Empire Trail
by Mary Anna Scenga Kruch

Two notes lead me to follow the arc
of a red-winged blackbird
through a stand of beech-maple and
white pines, my partner having rushed
on without me; I did not rush
to catch up, instead strayed further
from the path to explore
then was swept up in the lovely
chorus of C majors harmonizing
as they have done for centuries
in this fine, northernmost forest
the music moving me to pause
allowing it to seep into brittle bones
and to massage my knotted soul
caused me to hum notes that
I had abandoned long ago
all the way to the meeting place
where I'd not been missed and
no one waited to shepherd me home
so my old, tired feet dragged a little
as I swished through faded brown leaves
and worn-out weeds to the trailhead
where I raised my eyes to find two cranes
in perfect flight with two notes
seamlessly metered bugle calls
as they soared together homeward
and I set off alone toward mine.

Unfrozen
by Eileen Nittler

"There is not one right way
to care for yourself, other
than to listen to what you
need to do at that moment."
~ Eileen Nittler

When I was young, my knee-jerk reaction to stress was to freeze. It still is.
I was 10 and helping out a neighbor. She rightfully chastised me about something stupid I did. In response, I tiptoed out the back door and hid in the backyard.
I was 16 and at a party when my brain told me to move away from that boy, but my body froze instead.
I was 41 and lost my two daughters at the beach. For several minutes I stood rooted and panicking while I scanned the ocean. It did not occur to me to yell for help.
I was 57 and the presidential election sent me reeling. I can't freeze anymore.

We have all heard about Fight or Flight, Freeze or Flock. All of these are reasonable responses that serve a purpose. I am not dismissing the need to leave an unsafe situation, nor the tendency to shut down under stress, nor the desire to manically clean or knock back a shot of tequila or punch a pillow.

You do what you need to do.

In November:
I screamed at a man in public in a beach town in Colombia who was harassing me. That was self-care.
I doom-scrolled on Reddit all night. Also self-care, sort of.
I did 1000 sit-ups while on my back in a sunbeam. Double the self-care.

There is not one right way to care for yourself, other than to listen to what you need to do at that moment.

In December:
I wrote to my newly elected Senator.
I went for a long walk in a forest and appreciated the trees.
I scheduled a dentist appointment.

In January:
I started doom scrolling, only to realize that it was not working for me, and instead limited my social media use.
I called my mother and told her I loved her.
And she told me she loved me.

In February:
I will doom scroll a little bit.
I will help others to care for themselves.
I will fight and flock and maybe flee sometimes.
And I will care about myself and our world enough to not freeze anymore.

Your Enjoyment Removed
by Fara Bommarito

Only water and bar soap will be allowed to wash my face
But for now, I'll use my L'aneige Rejuvenating Undereye Cream
Hoping that I can fill the lines that have formed
Beneath my plain, dull, brown eyes

I'll be able to stop them from ripping out of my bone-showing, red
and blue veined fingers, the way I prep and poise myself for the
perception of others

for your goddamn enjoyment
I sleep with a bonnet, safely protecting the luscious hair
You wind up in your hand
To keep me at your side like a leash

For your fucking enjoyment
I rip layers of my skin off
To be smooth for your coarse hands
That will never understand
That your aftershave will never be taken away

"…that I would seize power in a bloody coup, that I would stop feeling manipulated, that I would take charge of my life, that I would stop saying that unconditional yes."
~ Deborah Blenkhorn

Leap
by Brooke Bianchi-Pennington

My life was a constant
Seeking,
Swinging,
From life-line to life-line.
Life-vine clinging,
Escaping the sinking.

But it was also a weaving.
So many lines in hand,
Planted and plaited,
Created,
A soft place to land.

Now, from home I watch
Others' confident hops
Leaping from tops
Of cozy nests,
So sure of twigs
To return to.

On the difference I dwell,
Forgetting I, too,
Have a well from which to draw,
Running deep,
Steeped,
With many hands along the way.

Before, each chasm crossed
Was no choice of mine.
Vine to crumbling vine,
Momentum moved me.

Now, just beyond my warm windows'
    weave,
A rustling in the leaves,
A call to believe,
That I, too, deserve A
leap of faith.
Not just
A jump of escape.

...cont'd. from page 24

K: And do you see your poetry as a tool for social change, especially regarding women's rights?

S: I don't know if it is a tool, but I know it can be. This is me now assuming that my poetry has that power, which I guess anybody's work can have. Can my poems move people? Over the years, many have messaged me about a few of my poems saying they've been touched, or moved by them, or the poem made them think deeply about the topic. So can they be tools? Yes, they can be. Are they? I don't know.

K: I think they probably are. So you do all of these things - manage a jewellery business, write, edit, run an online magazine - then on top of that, you do fundraising primarily for women and children in Afghanistan. How did you get into that?

S: This is a story I love to tell because, to so many, it sounds quite absurd. I've lived with chronic health issues for over 20 years, some of which impact my life on a daily basis. Around seven-odd years back, I was going through a very tough time for various reasons. I had faced a series of challenges, especially during my second pregnancy and after the birth of my son in 2011. He was quite a sick child until he turned four. During these years, my health deteriorated as well, mainly because I wasn't receiving the right medical help.

I've always been a reader; books have always been my happy place, but for years, I had barely read apart from the odd book here and there. And I think at a very low point, I expressed to one of my friends that I really just needed a good book. I was craving books that would give me company during this difficult phase. She recommended a few authors, including Afghan-American author Nadia Hashimi.

I read two of Nadia's books, and both had a profound impact on me at that time. While I didn't entirely draw parallels with the stories, I connected deeply with the characters. The Afghan culture and the Indian culture do have some similarities as well. Her books were a game-changer for me. They were soul-stirring and, in many ways, helped me begin my journey back to myself.

I read her books in 2019, and COVID started a few months later. Many of Nadia's author events transitioned online, and I made it a point to join as many as I could, time permitting. If you've heard her speak, you know she is an impressive speaker. As I listened to her back then, I remember thinking that, first, I hadn't been part of conversations that truly moved me in a long time, and second, here was someone I didn't know who shared the same values I believed in. For many years, I had felt a significant void in my life where conversations about meaningful topics were missing.

When I started *Coffee and Conversations*, I reached out to her for an interview, which raised a lot of interest in her here in Hong Kong once it was published. Book clubs and other groups contacted me to connect with Nadia. By August 2021, we had been in communication over various things. When the Taliban took over, for anybody connected to Afghanistan and her people, it felt like 9/11 all over again. It was hard to believe this was happening...I couldn't believe the world would allow this to happen. That was literally how I felt.

I remember calling up a friend of mine, saying, "I have to do something...I can't just sit and not do anything." I decided to start a Facebook group called *Hong Kong for Afghanistan*, where, in addition to sharing news, I reached out to people, particularly within the small business community, to raise funds for Afghan women. Over 50 businesswomen in Hong Kong joined the effort, including home-run businesses, candlemakers, yoga teachers, artists, designers, teachers, photographers, jewellery designers, nutritionists, bookstores, etc. Everybody donated a product or a service, and together we raised nearly $10,000 US Dollars within a few months.

A few months later, I reached out to Nadia Hashimi to ask if we could organize two online events with her to raise funds. I was confident that people would love listening to her speak and would contribute because she is intelligent and well-informed, and an excellent conversationalist - plus her books are fantastic. People from all over the world joined in, and together, the events raised just over $10,000 USD for Afghan widows and children.

While the author and her books aren't the reason I continue to advocate for Afghan women and children, they were certainly the reason I felt the call to do something as deeply as I did in 2021.

In 2023, I started making candles for charity, a hobby I picked up during the COVID lockdown. I realised I could use this hobby to raise funds, which I've been doing for the past two years. A fundraiser that was originally intended to last one month is still active after three years. People often ask me how long I will continue this work, and my response is always the same: I will continue till I'm effective.

K: And is there a specific organisation, or organisations that you donate to?

S: So, right at the start, I reached out to Nadia on social media (as did many of her readers) and chose an organization from the list she and the Afghan American Foundation had shared. I always knew I didn't want to go with the big organizations, like Red Cross or the WHO. I believe in grassroots-level work, and I looked at who the Afghans trusted with their aid money. Some Afghans who left the country started their own organisations, and these are the ones who are able to really go door to door to deliver aid. I reached out to each of the organizations I wanted to donate to, spoke to their founders and team members. Kirsty, for me, a lot of the work has also been about maintaining these relationships, building a community, because for grassroots-level work, you just can't donate to an organisation and forget. If I'm trying to get food, sanitary aid and help into people's homes, and I need proof that the aid is reaching them, I need an organisation that can do that. I've chosen organisations that the Afghan community and the diaspora trust.

K: That's amazing! What are the names of the organisations?

S: The one that I am doing most of my current aid work through is Hope and Kindness Afghanistan Organization. The founder's name is Khalyla Harito, who is an amazing Afghan woman. She left the country after the Taliban took over, and serves as the patron of two orphanages I support in Kabul. Her grass-roots organization helps with everything

Upper left: Food distribution to Afghan Widows

Below: Food, blanket and household items donated with Home renovations

Lower left: Sewing machine and food distribution to Afghan widows

from direct food aid to job carts for families and setting up sewing machines for under-privileged women. In February and early March we did a sanitary aid drive for over 170 women and girls.

Two other organizations which we've donated to and have global recognition are Aseel and Help Build Tomorrow.

K: I think also, since you had such a success in the first fundraising like you said, all those women joined together in the very beginning. I think that's also a sign, really, or synchronicity, that this is something that is important for, not just for Afghanistan but for the progression of women's liberation, you know, because I believe in that statement, we're not free until we're all free. And also, what happens in Afghanistan could very easily and quickly happen anywhere. I mean, they're trying to do it in America. Right?

And do you think that storytelling and poetry play a role in raising awareness about the plight of Afghan women?

S: Yes. I'm sitting here, doing what I'm doing essentially because of two books I read. I read about Afghan women's plight in books written by an Afghan woman, who really conveyed the stories the way they're meant to be conveyed - with authenticity (and beautiful prose I might add). That's why they moved me. The creative arts are effective tools for raising awareness, and play a huge role in fostering empathy and connecting people.

K: What were Nadia's books that you read? What were their titles? You said you read two of them.

S: *A House Without Windows*, and *The Pearl that Broke its Shell*. For anyone reading this and is familiar with Nadia Hashimi's work, the much awaited sequel to *The Pearl that Broke its Shell*, titled *City of Widows* comes out in 2026. Can you tell I'm excited!

K: And then my final question, what message do you hope to send to the Afghan women through your work?

S: Unless my message can directly impact their lives, I don't believe Afghan women—particularly those we have been helping—can benefit much from just receiving messages. What can I really say to them? I will never completely understand their lives and hardships, and it would be highly insensitive of me to even pretend I can. Afghan women need this dysfunctional, dangerous and dystopian world they have been forced into to change, and I have no political influence and can't help with that.

From day one, I have focused on delivering aid; that's where I've directed my energy, and honestly, I have never thought about anything else. I will add, though, that I've been told that a few women and girls we've helped feel supported and cared for, and a little less alone in their fight. While I haven't sent any specific message through my work, I believe that's the message they have received.

***

You can learn more about Shikha at one of the links below:

Poetry - www.instagram.com/shikhaslambapoetry
Magazine - www.coffeeandconversations.in
Website - www.shikhaslamba.com

And here are the links for the organisations Shikha supports:

Hope and Kindness Afghanistan - https://www.instagram.com/hope.kindness.afg/
Aseel - https://aseelapp.com/
Help Build Tomorrow - https://hbt.org/

Left: Sewing machine and food distribution to Afghan widows

Right: Home renovations for Afghan widows

"I came to realize that the
best self-care is not
found in a cup or a tub. I
found it on planes and
cruise ships. A week away
somewhere exotic is
unfathomably healing."
~ Ginger Strivelli

Travel is the Best Self-Care
by Ginger Strivelli

For a quarter of a century, I was raising my six children, three of whom are autistic. I was my children's full-time caregiver. I was a part-time caregiver for my amputee grandfather, then my elderly grandmother, then my mother. I was a housekeeper and homemaker. I was an aspiring writer and artist. I was active in my religious community. Everyone always told me that I had my hands full.

My hands, head, and heart were full of stress. I always said that I ate stress for breakfast. Back then, no one talked about self-care or me-time. I still learned those skills that hadn't been named yet. I had to practice those coping techniques. Caregiver burnout was also not discussed back then. Nonetheless, I was suffering from it.

Self-care is all the rage now. All our rage, anxiety, depression and stress are why we need to be taken care of, and alas, oftentimes, we can only count on ourselves to care. That is where I was for all those years. I practiced self-care even if we didn't call it that yet. I sipped hibiscus tea to calm my nerves. I took my prescribed meds to battle the panic attack anxiety disorder and PTSD that I suffered from. I popped melatonin to get to sleep and chugged southern sweet tea to wake myself up after getting too little sleep. I chanted Om Shanti for my fifteen minutes of peace when I could find fifteen minutes to do so. I prayed often and studied holy books from every ancient culture on Mother Earth. I took scorching baths to relax my achy muscles. I constantly nibbled on chocolate to fight off migraines and sadness. However, I was still too often stressed and depressed.

I came to realize that the best self-care is not found in a cup or a tub. I found it on planes and cruise ships. A week away somewhere exotic is unfathomably healing. It healed my body, mind, and soul. Traveling the world once a year or so saved my life during those busy years. That is not hyperbole.

I had to save my nickels and dimes up daily for months and months to afford it, but it was so worth it. The joys of planning for, packing for, and going on those adventures are what kept me sane and coping reasonably well for all those years that I ate stress for breakfast.

I went to India, Greece, Mexico, Egypt, The Bahamas, Rome, and Belize. Those trips were what I paced myself towards as I stumbled through my stressful day-to-day life as Super Caregiver, complete with a cape and tiara. Looking forward to traveling was my daily motivation to keep going and see the bright side, even on dark days.

Alas, out of the blue, my stressful but managed life went completely sideways. My husband left me on the eve of our twenty-sixth anniversary.

My two neurotypical daughters were away at college. I was alone with my three disabled children and my younger neurotypical son. He was in high school, working a fast-food job, and in the marching band. He didn't have time to take care of me. As usual, no one was taking care of me. I was still taking care of everyone else somehow.

When the smoke cleared, I knew what I had to do to get through it, recover, and heal. I had to take care of myself and travel. My older grown children all finally didn't need me twenty-four-seven. My youngest daughter was a teen but was autistic and did still need me to be her full-time caregiver. I told myself, her, and everyone else that she and I were moving to Egypt. No one believed me. They all said I couldn't, shouldn't, wouldn't.

On my forty-sixth birthday, my fourteen-year-old autistic daughter and I moved to Luxor, Egypt, the ancient city that the Pharaohs called Thebes. We did her home schoolwork in the three-thousand-year-old temple of Ramses the Great, in the Roman-era temple of the Goddess Isis in the Sahara Desert, and in the other temples and tombs that were within a mile or two from our new home. My daughter and I were actually living in ancient Thebes by the River Nile.

We even traveled while we were living there in Luxor. We traveled back and forth to the States for the holidays, visiting my grown kids. We traveled by car and train and plane, visiting the magical other Egyptian cities of Cairo, Giza, Alexandria, Dendera, Abydos, Philae, and Saqqara. My daughter did her homeschool lessons, and I drew, wrote, quilted, and painted in ancient magical sites all over Egypt. We

learned to speak Arabic. I had a pet baby camel. She had a pet donkey. We lived in Egypt for two and a half epic years before we had to move back to the States.

Alas, I can't travel as far and wide now as I did back then. I don't have the financial means to travel as often or as far anymore. I hope to get back to globe-trotting soon because I really need to. However, these days, I am having to make do with lesser acts of self-care. I use the chocolate, the chanting, and all the little things we tell each other to do to fight caregiver burnout and other stresses of unfair life. They help some, but traveling helps more.

Now, with a more modest traveling budget, I have found an Alien Space Conference in my state to spend a weekend away at, as well as a city an hour away holding an Octoberfest. I visited a Hindu temple outside of Atlanta, like the ones I love to visit on my trips to India.

Even during the worst of the COVID epidemic in 2020, I drove to the coast and communed with the mystical sea Gods along with three of my daughters for a few days. We stayed in a deserted hotel on a very unpopulated beach. We went midweek and didn't eat in restaurants or go around anyone but each other on the trip, so we were able to travel safely. I also went to Judaculla Rock trail, an outdoor site with an ancient rock with mysterious petroglyphs in Cherokee, NC, that I'd never gotten to before.

I can now take little road trips to nearby sites. I could take a bus or train to some place further away that I've not seen yet. Even when I can't travel to some Renaissance Faire or Comic Con an hour to two away, I can still practice travel self-care. I can plan a Hawaiian weekend right in my home. I can pick up books about Hawaii from the library. I can download Hawaiian music and documentaries to

enjoy. I can line up a TV show set in Hawaii to binge binge-watch. I can rent a couple of movies about Hawaiian history. I can pick up a pineapple, a coconut, and a can of Spam to make Hawaiian food and drinks. I can spend the weekend exploring Hawaii from my home sweet home in North Carolina.

I've learned that traveling is the best self-care. Sometimes, you just have to get away. You have to learn about other languages, cultures, and religions. You need to explore and have adventures. Seize the day. When in Rome, do as the Romans do. Even if it is just Rome, Georgia or a Roman culture fest you've planned to enjoy in your living room this weekend.

Travel as much, as often, and as far as you can for your own well-deserved self-care.

***

Quieting
by Kirk Lawson

Snowflakes collect on a skylight,
random yet not
create a balanced
steady landscape

thousands of crisp flakes
stacked, layered, resting
each a part of a larger whole
adding up to

a thick comfort that
soothes and envelops
a cloak of calm
quiets the racing self

a hush takes my breath away
stops me from muttering
words that might harm
or create dis-ease

a salve that shields
my ears from noise
to pollute the soul
instead a healing music

a silence that prevents
anger from taking over
stems brewing temper
creates calm acceptance

a centering peace
that focusses my vision
removes obstacles
so I see clearly

reminds me
I am alive
breathing, feeling
seeing, grateful

blanketed in peace
and gratitude.

"Self–esteem and self–love are the opposites of fear; the more you like yourself, the less you fear anything."
~ Brian Tracy

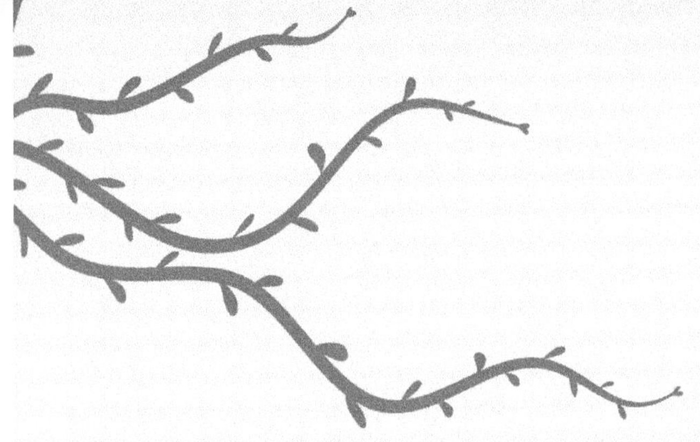

Letters To My Therapist
by Hunter Hays

Dear Joanna,

I know that there is a lot to unpack. Maybe I should just focus on one thing at a time? Until I started talking, I didn't realize how many people had hurt me...or how bad it made them sound when I finally said it out loud. In a lot of ways, I'm still trying to untie all the knots in the story, following strands I forgot about, and unlocking memories; I want to have a clearer picture.

Dear Joanna,

You asked me once what I would have said to them if I had the chance. You suggested I write letters to them, unfiltered, uncensored. That's harder than I expected. I wrote several of them to different people, but a letter felt too personal. It made me feel too exposed. I instead chose to write these letters to you. It's a way to process without confronting the people who have hurt me directly, as well as serve as a reminder of either what we have already covered or should cover. Though, I will admit I kept a few of the old letters. I turned those into stories. In some cases, they were just accounts of what happened. In other cases they were imaginings I had while healing. Even though the stories and letters were so different, I found myself asking the same questions every time.

Dear Joanna,

Do you believe in ghosts?
What is it like to not be afraid to say goodbye?
Is being loved supposed to hurt?
How can I be sure being hurt wasn't my fault?
Why does the girl crying in the mirror look like I did when I was eight?
Why does my brain make me want to dive into the water and never come up for air?
Why did they hurt me?
Why did they hurt me?

Dear Joanna,

Am I a coward for being too afraid to say goodbye? I don't think I feel like I want to end my life anymore… just for a moment, I wish the sounds in my head would go away. I want the white noise to stop buzzing, Little Me's crying out for Mommy to cease, my heart to stop hurting. I'll be real, I didn't think I would make it this far. I thought I would be long gone by fifteen and definitely before twenty-seven. I am thirty and now I don't know what to do. I don't want to be strong. I want to have been able to break down and have a safe place to do so. I wanted to be able to run home to my mom when someone hurt me. I wanted to be able to tell the truth about everything.

I don't want to lie to people and pretend that everything is fine. It wasn't. Sure, there were good moments, birthdays, and sleepovers, and parties - but I can't remember most of them other than what I see in leftover pictures.

I've seen pictures of me doing dishes, smiling half-heartedly at the camera, with my purple sweater and denim pleated skirt (no one said I was stylish, okay?), standing in front of the blue speckled counters and slightly crooked white cabinets that did their best to match the white and brown tiles that made up the floor. When I see the picture, I remember the glasses broken in the sink, being pushed and tripping over the dishwasher, and crying on the floor by the cupboards when I was home alone.

There is a picture of me and a girl I went to high school with making silly faces in my room. The walls are nauseating (foot-wide stripes of orange, blue, pink, and green), and everything is bright. We are laughing and sticking our tongues out. What I remember is hiding in my room, barricading my door with my dresser until my dad got after me for a "fire hazard".

I remember taking my little brother into his room after being told by my mom, "If anything happens, call 911." I distracted him while they screamed at each other in the kitchen.
My brother got scared at some point, but I took the batteries out of the phone so he couldn't call. Unfortunately, I had been trained well by that point. I still hate myself a little for that one.

My childhood feels tainted with silently wondering if anyone has figured out what happened. I spent so long lying to myself and to everyone around me because I didn't want to get my family in trouble. I was conditioned to protect them at the cost of my own sanity.

I want to rewrite what happened. I want to forget the face of every person who has assaulted or harassed me. I want to not freak out any time I think I see a former assailant across the grocery store. I don't want to have to play pretend anymore. I think most of all what I want is to stop feeling so angry. I don't know what to do with all this hate. I hate how he touched me. I hate how she covered for him. I hate that he either doesn't remember or doesn't care. I can't figure out which is worse.

Dear Joanna,

I know that there is an end to everything. I will graduate soon; will die eventually...How do I know when therapy is over? There is no certificate for healing from trauma. No grade point average I can look at and feel validated knowing that I no longer have to be scared of running into him in public. There is nothing to frame and display on a mantle to show that dealing with the trauma from when I was seven is starting to hurt less every day. How wonderful it may be when I graduate from therapy. Maybe I'll be able to talk to them then.

Dear Joanna,

No one told me that healing was going to hurt so much. It's like all the pieces of me are being jammed back together, but after years of smoothing out sharp and jagged edges to make myself smaller and easier to handle, things are hard to put back together. Time keeps moving forward, whether I have healed fully or not. I don't have to keep anyone's secrets. I can be honest with myself and with you. I can admit that I was hurt. Really hurt. In some ways, I still am. I can't change what happened, and I am slowly learning that I am still okay. I still deserve to be here. I am still here. I am looking forward to what comes next.

I feel, dare I say, hopeful.

***

Liberty has Pace
by Glenn Marchand

It may be cold sensitivity, angry compassion. It may be hell in winter, raw cadence. A man to his thoughts, sin to its body, excellence to its cages—a soul confined to one region, unthought by

discomfort, assumed as preferential. So terrible for breath, too misunderstood, a man is ever wrong, nudgingly intrusive, anxiety compulsive. To have loved was outstanding, those rich moments, to purchase moons, to besprinkle stars, such celestial passions—life of one's depth, death of one's fears, to have possessed what seems to perish. And prose is tragic, our eyes darting, our souls

cutting, a short run of perfection. (If it isn't light, it's darkness, it's marbled—such longing liberation, the freedom of attraction.) A world trying to break webs, by grace, by sacrifice, if to sound out one's voice—if anything good might hurt us, if feelings were pillars—to offer sanity, to bestow upon us safety. It was meant to ensure prosperity, wilderness isn't affection, to take

courage, to nurture an endless vine, to nibble a heart-shaped fig. Motion is courage, asking for cosmic translation, molded to treasure sunshine. What becomes special are eyes probing innocence; indeed, an antiquated ideal—our pace is legendary, fraught by fragility. Hands to crocheting. Measure of self-affection; to adore appetite, careful to apply love.

Feminist is the New F Word
Says The Hardcore, Placard-carrying Feminist in 6 Stanzas and Two Equations
by Kasimma

I don't know what my best colour is, but I know it is not white. White is a gossip, no, not a gossip—at least a gossip gossips while telling themselves that they are not gossiping—a busybody. Clerics wear white clothes to show their cleanliness, piousness, next-to-Godliness.

1.

Abuja downtown has electricity and water supply, smooth and wide roads, edifices with luxury roofs, malls, diri gabazie. As one proceeds to its uptowns, the scene dwindles to heating ordinariness. The estate where I lived is on the rumpled side of the downtown coin. Rows of bushes flank columns of red earth between. When the sea's roof cries, cars get trapped in mud. Since the outset of the estate, and I have no idea when that was, men have been chairpersons: Estate Officials, they are called. During the campaign of the outgoing chairman, he and two of his friends knocked on doors bright and early in the a.m. one Saturday. People cheered and supported him. Enter 2020. A woman declared interest in the chairmanship position and da-bloooood-of-Jesus! Our once-mute WhatsApp group flooded with mouths beefy with smelly prejudice for her. Nobody else declared interest in this position or any position for that matter. She typed up a manifesto, made a flyer, campaigned! She even invoked her Ph.D. and her husband's testimony of support for her agenda. All this aplomb for an unpaid, unwanted, unopposed position! Yet,

a character called Izik goes back to the history of our WhatsApp group and screenshot chats where she promises to download God's vomit on those people who choose to discuss loudly by her window at midnight and those who come to her house to destroy her lemongrass. Izik's low move brushed my tongue in coats of acrid blue. So, I responded:

There is nothing this woman has said or done that is evil, absolutely nothing. She will not be the first chairperson in this estate. But we have not had these many chats because of elections. Izik and others who screenshot and posted her chats are not angels. We are all flawed. Every single one of us is flawed. And nobody has a single story. She is flawed too. She has her bad and good sides like the rest of us. I wonder why you people are focusing on a negative single story. If God should look at our sins, who will survive? As far as I am concerned, the only crime she committed is being a woman. **This is the reason you all want to crucify her and tear down her person.**

Well, the busybody, Izik, groaned a pathetic, supposedly admonitory, kumbaya of how irritating my comment is, how the problem with feminists is that they go about looking for trouble and scattering people's homes, how blah-blah-black-sheep-have-you-any-wool. Well, no, sir, no, sir, none for you!

2.

I have a dear cousin whom I shall call Y. Her bold eyes and her upper incisor, which is missing an arc of a tooth, enlighten her smile. Y would lift a baked stone with her bare palms if that'd save another woman from trouble. Y has little patience for men's tantrums. Y agrees with the sentiments of feminism. She upholds and defends them furiously. Yet, when I called her a feminist, she crumpled like rumpled chiffon. "Aw-shucks, I am not a feminist!" It appeared Y was saying, "Be polite; don't use the F-word! Don't stain my white!"

"Fuck" is one of the juiciest fruits on the tree of words. One likes it; one should not eat it. "Fuck" is an all-encompassing word. "Fuck you" does not mean "have sex you" it can mean "go-to-hell you" or "leave-me-alone you" or "I-don't-care you." Fuck makes its recipients push back.

> "Colonization was endured until the people said no. Things just don't happen; people make them happen."
> ~ Kasimma

a. *Rudeness + Politeness = Nkapi*
   if Rudenss = Fuck you
   and Politeness = F you
   then ≈ Fuck you ≠ F you
   ∴ Fuck you + F you = Nkapi

Qed.

Nkapi, the Shrew Rat, finds human feet attractive. It bites and puffs its victim's foot simultaneously so that they don't feel the discomfort of its bites. I see Nkapi when someone, in reaching for clean language, says "F you" instead of "fuck you". If you think it and proceed to open your mouth to utter it, be, at the very least, bold enough to say what you want to say. "F you" doesn't make the taste less unpleasant.

b. *Feminist you ≥ Fuck you*

$$\frac{feminist\ \cancel{(you)}}{\cancel{you}} \geq \frac{Fuck\ \cancel{(you)}}{\cancel{you}}$$

≈ Feminist ≥ Fuck

Qed.

Feminist is greater than or equal to Fuck you, not simply equal to, because it now seems as though being called a feminist carries more baggage than "fuck you." If someone says, "Fuck you" to the Ys— it doesn't matter if their act at that time deserves an overwhelmingly decorated fuck-you—they might say, "Fuck you too," or anything other than shrinking and saying, "I am not a fuck-you." But call them feminists and da-bloooood-of-Jesus! How dare you tinge their white!!!

Ladies and gentlemen of the jury, I am pleased to inform you that the new F-word is "Feminist". (Go on, don't be shy to applaud!)

3.

Do you smell it, the idiocy boiling in misogyny? Women have sunk to their graves on the weight of blames that rightfully belongs to men. Women are blamed for "getting" raped, blamed for "getting" beat up by their husbands, blamed for their husbands' infidelity, blamed when their children turn out bad. Blamed! You smell it now, don't you, the nzuzu boiling in misogyny? Women are made to feel as though they are the <u>only</u> ones subsumed in the orchestra of marriage, as though marriage is a mere inconvenience to the man. Igbo people say that marriage is a woman's crown. What type of crown, pray tell? When women complain that the crown of thorns is making them bleed, they are shushed: *Be happy you even have a crown! Did Jesus complain about his own crown?* Why involve Jesus in this issue, I wonder? Did Jesus' crucifixion certificate say, "Hereabove crucified is Jesus, the Married Woman"? Men who think misogyny profits them are sunk in cocoons of illusion. Women and men suffer from misogyny.

Do you smell it yet, the idiocy boiling in misogyny? Perceive this: how about we tell men to excuse their bodies of their instruments of rape and infidelity, penises and fingers, instead of telling girls to avoid "getting" raped. Oh, shall we amputate Mr. Man's hands or better still relieve his skull of his unused brain so that it doesn't even occur to him to beat his woman? Inanity, right? Good. But those people who push for love-thy-neighbour-as-thou-loveth-thyself are now called troublemakers, bad people, who want to scatter families. You smell it now, don't you, the iberibe boiling in misogyny? My comment sent Izik's intention, to showcase that woman as a vicious person, gathering itself into an apt countenance of thank-you-and-bye-bye. His comeback, having negotiated the lump of maggoty misogyny he mistakes for an Adam's apple, oozing of pong asininity, was an effort to salvage whatever was left of his pauci-dignity. His groan of helpless disheartenment was in service of shielding his white.

4.

Newton's first law states that: *the velocity of an object will not change unless the object is acted on by an outside force.* The foremost step in battle is to buy a lead by hoodwinking the other through lauding lies until it becomes a recurring song in their heads and, in effect, their truth. Change happens when people shrink the velocity of those lies to a stop, when people strip those lies of their

tie to gravity so that they can float to oblivion. There was a time when slavery was legal until some slaves said no. It took decades of force and blood, but now slavery is synonymous with hellfire. Apartheid was suffered by South Africans until the people pushed back. Colonization was endured until the people said no. Things just don't happen; people make them happen. Let it not be said that I am advocating for violence, no. I abhor violence.

I have survived the devilry of domestic violence of the physical, psychological, economic, financial, verbal, (name-it!) variant. I have literally shed blood and tears. Violence is not even funny. People with whom I share love have scalded me in deep ways for being a feminist. I don't hate them. Hatred cannot extinguish hatred. Instead, I pity them because they are products of a society that teaches them to demean women. Regardless of the scars, I am still an unshakable, hardcore, placard-carrying feminist. What doesn't set you back propels you forward. Now, when I peep into my chalice of blood to shed, of tears to cry, of hurts to feel, of fucks to give, I find it shiningly empty.

When African Americans boycotted buses and trekked miles to work, they did so, not for themselves, but for their children and unborn children. When Ruby Bridges became the first person-of-colour to attend an all person-of-no-colour public William Frantz Elementary School, she and her parents did it for the African race. When Rosa Parks refused to give up her seat on the bus, she was thinking of Emmett Till, not herself. So, who am I to say that because I am persecuted for my belief, I'd hang them on the gust of forgetfulness? Ha! I ga-askiwa! A killed person cannot be killed. I will only get louder in this struggle, for equality, for world peace, for my children.

5.

Since Feminism is the new F-word, it is difficult now to be called a feminist. That is why Y pushed back on the word, never mind that she and feminism are like apple and apple skin. I did not sink into bedazzling disbelief when Izik threw the new F-word at me. Fighting him will solve nothing; offing misogyny will. Contrary to what Izik expects of me, to hide my white cloak from stains, me who does not even wear white, I am reiterating to him and the world that I, Kasimma, am a hardcore, placard-carrying feminist. I matter. I belong to, and am beneath, no one. *Peereeiod*! I salute Frances Ogamba, Mubanga Kalimamukwento, Chika Unigwe, Chimamanda Ngozi Adichie, Ukamaka Olisakwe, feminists whose pens scoop the sunlight and spread it on pages of enlightenment, vanquishing the whispering of machismo history and turning it to melodic herstory. I had, with the deepest appreciation, applied Ms. Adichie's words in my response to Izik's sorry shenanigans.

When a drum of water has dirt settled underneath, and someone scoops a cup carefully so as not to unsettle the dirt, that person is, willy-nilly, still drinking dirty water. Is it not better to pour the dirty water away, wash the drum, and refill it with clean water? Dirt cannot wipe itself. Someone must do the cleaning. An unhappy family is already a scattered family. Feelings are intrusive. If we have forced colonization, slavery, into the grave, we must also banish sexism into the same grave and make strong efforts to cover that grave! The pelting rains of misogyny must surrender to the tranquil reigns of feminism. Women must strip themselves of the white cloak of cleanliness, piousness, next-to-Godliness. Women are not angels. Women are not clerics. Women are simply women.

My hope is that the world will be free from the suffocating cage of misogyny.

6.

Ọgwụ go kwa ka ọ ra m n'ọnụ, at least for now. Feminist is the new f-word. So go ahead; don't be polite; use the new F-word. Don't be ashamed of being called a feminist.

Need I say more?

***

Where.
by Daniel Barry

where is one to go to find care?
under a shell?
a care that exists
beyond a five second sales pitch.

when one's mother has
died, and you've taken
your PTO, where is one to go???
when the fire shows his shaggy head

and you have not charged
your extinguishers;
and small animals have thrown
themselves into their trenches;

and it rains to no avail;
and someone brutal kicks you
from a dark corner,
imparting a limp.

the archetypal eyes of evil
are not merely imagined;
they require the zeal of one
locked in a room with a keyboard

to summon and some have dedicated their lives
to acquire them.
and among these things,
a free cup of coffee on the jubilant eve

of the second coming,
the sun, gushing over the horizon
among easy clouds,
reminding you of the majesty of having eyes.

and tell me, child,
can such a being of both worlds
ever find care?
and if so, where?

Journey to Myself
by Lena Samson

I grew up desperate for love and acceptance. My immigrant parents, traumatized by war and resettlement in a foreign culture, had no time in their lives for affection. Life was about struggling, working, fighting to survive. No time for fun, no place for hugs, no appreciation for accomplishments. No support. My brothers and I were fed and clothed; the rest was up to us.

I could do nothing right around my mother. She insulted, condescended, and was not able to help me fit into the Western culture that she didn't understand. She wanted me to hide away from it, to acquiesce to her culture—one that I did not see around me and did not understand. In her world, singing in the house was a sin; whistling at the table was a sin. Meanwhile, I was learning in school and on television to be kind to each other and treat people with respect. There was no respect in my house. I was confused.

Despite all this negativity, I felt that I was a good person. A quiet, shy girl, I became a smart student and relished any praise given by my teachers. School became a haven where I could be accepted. When I brought home A's on my report card, my mother just laughed. She was not able to help with anything school-related since she was uneducated and barely spoke English. I learned to be ashamed of her, unable to attend parent-teacher interviews like other parents or contribute to my school life in any meaningful way. She couldn't even write my absence notes—I had to print them in my childish hand while she learned to carefully script the letters that formed her name. My teachers knew that I had written the notes, and I was ashamed.

A kind, caring girl, I was eager to make friends. I did what I was told and never made trouble. That was still not good enough for my mother. I never understood what she expected of me. I think I was supposed to fly under the radar and not be noticed, akin to how my parents survived in this world. Going unnoticed helped them to survive war, and it was how they would get by on this side of the ocean. When I became a teenager and boys became attracted to me, their plans would fail. My parents didn't want me to date, which, of course, was completely unrealistic. I found boyfriends, and that was the start of my troubles.

The lack of love that I felt from my parents translated into an unhealthy need to find love elsewhere. I was honest and trusting—when a boy or man said they loved me, I believed them. I so desperately needed to hear it, to feel it. I treated people the way I wanted to be treated and thought that others were the same. Foolish me. My mom was no help, of course; she had trapped my father into marrying her so she could have children. I had no one to give me direction or advice.

And so, I'd attach myself to a partner, ecstatic that the world would finally see that I was loved, that I was worthwhile. I suffered from society's message that a woman was only valued if she had a man. And yet, I was intelligent, funding my way through university against the wishes of my parents. My father said I was "stupid" to want a higher education since I would just get married and have children. Therefore, my driving force in life became to prove him wrong. I would graduate and earn a fulfilling career, showing him that he underestimated me, that his thinking was backward and old-fashioned. I would do it my way.

And I did. But that need to be loved never left me. I married an older man who worked in my office, and we had two wonderful children. But we were at different stages of our lives—I wanted to travel, experience the world, learn and move up in my career while he was happy staying still. Our love was not lasting, if it was ever love in the first place. I certainly had no examples to follow as my parents never seemed to even like each other. I had sworn to myself that I would never put my children through the kind of childhood I had, full of anger, yelling and insults. If my husband and I were to stop getting along, I would divorce so my children would benefit from two happy parents apart as opposed to two miserable ones together.

Yet, as a single parent, I continued to pursue the type of relationship I read about and saw on TV. I wanted someone who loved only me, longed for only me—a partner who would put me first above all else. I was not happy dating as I didn't feel safe and longed for one person who would give me the security and unflinching love that I craved. So, I embarked on a second marriage with a man who was very different from my first husband, an even bigger mistake. I tried for years to endure and make it work. I swore I wouldn't get a second divorce. My parents stayed together for the children, and I would do the same.

But it became intolerable, and I had to leave. I had kept my misery to myself, ashamed to admit that this marriage was not working. My pride was too great, making me need to show the world that I was normal and in a committed relationship. I suffered and suffered. After I moved out, a friend told me I looked like someone who was suddenly freed of a heavy, sodden wool coat that I had worn for ages. I was surprised that my desolation had been visible; I had worked so hard to hide it, to pretend I was happy.

On my own, I dated again, making the same mistakes over and over, trusting and believing. Still seeking that elusive happily-ever-after. My dream was to be part of a white-haired old couple someday, walking hand-in-hand. But I never knew how to look for a man who respected me, who adored who I was inside, who treasured my intelligence, my humour, my kindness and love. I never knew how to look or what to look for.

Finally, after a devastating relationship with a man who was a complete fraud, I gave up. By this time, my first granddaughter had been born, and I became committed to helping my daughter and spending as much time with this fledgling little life force as I could. I had become jaded, searching for an elusive partner, and began to feel that I didn't need that complication in my life. I was fine on my own; I could do what I wanted and be myself.

During my traumatic second divorce, I saw a psychologist for support and to help me understand everything I was going through. I started to read and seek answers to the questions as to why I couldn't find a lasting relationship. Professional counselling opened my eyes to my own critical reality, one that I had never understood: lacking the love I had needed as a child, I had sought that love from men. But they just saw my vulnerability and took advantage at every turn. I didn't know what it felt like to be respected and admired, so I couldn't seek it in my relationships.

I have been seeing a natural healing doctor for years. In one of our sessions, she did an emotional cleanse for me. Through the fascinating process, I found myself crying for no reason that I could understand. She told me that she saw many umbilical cords tying me to my mother and encouraged me to visualize throwing each one off, one at a time. I envisioned my entanglement in an octopus' tentacles and saw myself unwrapping each one and tossing it away. I began to understand how fiercely my mother had tied me to her, even after she had been dead for five years.

She had created this love/hate bond with me, whereby she was free to insult and put me down while I still cared for her in her old age, doing everything I could as a good daughter. My emotional cleanse helped me considerably; afterwards, when I visited my mother's grave, I felt a healthy distancing that I didn't know I needed.

And now, I have learned how critical self-care has been in my healing process. Psychologists, counsellors, books and other reference materials showed me that I had to fully arrive at a place where I could love myself, where I could be proud of my accomplishments and the wonderful children I have raised. I am blessed with three granddaughters who give me all the love I need in this world. I have nothing to prove to anyone.

I am happily retired, finding new purpose through my writing. Writing has enabled me to express my pain and my healing—it has birthed my voice that was suppressed from childhood. Poetry has emerged from all my sorrows and has lifted my soul. I take walks in the woods, embracing the scent of the trees, marvelling at the scurrying little animals, inhaling the forest's regenerating power. I have found new friendships with people who share my passion for writing. All of this has become my essential self-care. Never did I imagine I could arrive at such peace.

It has been a long journey—a lifelong journey--full of joy, pain and discovery. I have metaphorically cut myself open to learn my intrinsic truths, even when it hurts. But this learning has been essential and enabled me to blossom into the real me: the me that is happy with myself.

Finally.

***

"Any education given by a group
tends to socialise its members, but
the quality and value of the
socialisation depends on the
habits and aims of the group."
~ John Dewey

Within
by Deborah Le Falle

deep inside my soul
is a coveted, sacred space

it is where I go
when I want to *be* alone
with my authentic self and reflect

on things that bring me joy
being   alive and well
     appreciative of bare moments
          immersed in creativity
               enraptured in play
present with plants, birds
          in community with kindreds

it is a space I enter
to   converse with life
     seek guidance, justice
          tap into strength, wisdom
               unveil truth, light
embrace peace, love
          replenish my spirit

a simple, yet treasured space
for nourishing my vessel's
ever-evolving existence

I wonder when I'll be happy,
Deep in my chasm of despair.
I haven't got all I deserve.
My meagre lot does not compare.

I'm told it cannot be purchased,
that happiness comes from inside.
Build good habits.
Make good choices.
Things that only I can decide.

True,
I'm a flawed human being.
That is never going to alter.
I should show *me* more compassion
all those times I err and falter.

I'll replace that empty chasm
of bottomless expectation,
with contagious smiles that display
my thanks and appreciation.

I'll need a strong network of friends
for my happiness to succeed.
Then one day soon,
I might just find,
the life I have is all I need?

The Ivy's Grudge
by Steffi Kim

The woman has not spoken in forty-two days. She sits in her cell, back rigid against the cement wall. Fluorescent lights glare down on her angular face, her sallow eyes and pinched-in cheeks. She does not pace around like a caged animal. Some days, she gazes out the window like a bird with bridled wings, straining towards the sun. Most days, she just waits. Periodically, officers come in and interrogate her, gravelly demands scraping through the air. She stares them dead in the eye, refusing to answer a single word. They huff and sigh, fiddle with their badges and tear hands through their hair. Curse and spit. Rattle their handcuffs.

But in the end, there is nothing they can do.

The state has brought in psychologists, nurses, lawyers. One by one, they file into her cell. Drag a stool in front of her bench, the metal legs grating across the polished floor.

"Don't worry," the guards tell them, "She's not dangerous."

They scribble onto their notepads, scratching lines and arrows and question marks. Question marks. There are far too many of them. What truly happened that December night?

That night, where a cacophony of red and blue lights swept across the block, where sirens screamed, and neighbors awoke to dapples of scarlet. The sound of glass splintering against asphalt. The hiss of water being doused onto a burning house, saturating the ground until every last ember fizzled into darkness. The firefighters had braved the inferno. A father remained trapped inside, but it was too risky to save him. As for the mother, the police found her two towns away, wads of cash stashed in her jacket pockets. Found her kidnapping their two daughters.

Some say she is the framed victim; others say she is the perpetrator.

"The patient is perfectly sane," the psychologists have reported.

Detectives have opened her file countless times, poured over her background. Overexposed photos bulge from the manilla folder. She used to be so pretty when she was younger. How is it possible, they wondered, that such a nice girl could go so wrong?

If only they could stitch together the tatters of her life, they would emerge with a tapestry, a semblance, a specter of a woman. They would not see her in black and white, as an angel or a witch. They'd emerge with a pallet of poignant blues, caustic reds, rotted yellows, and ceaseless grays. Under her piercing stare, they would see a mosaic of hurt. Under her silent irises, they would grasp what she had been hiding from them all along. That once upon a time, she fell like snow from the heavens, untainted, untouched by this world. But the world had overwhelmed her, smothered her from the very start.

*

First, they told her to be a daisy. They swathed her in lacy blankets, placed a pink bonnet over her peachy face. Her upturned nose was brushed with coral, her cheeks were pale. They gazed at her with soft expressions, spoke to her in whispers, as if a loud noise could fracture her fragile frame. Her eyes were often squeezed tight; she was too pure for this world. But when her father sang, they fluttered open, and they soaked in the afternoon sunlight. Her grandmother cradled her, coddled her like a porcelain doll. Her mother pampered her, bathed her in buttermilk. When she cried,

they quickly shushed her, when she kicked, they shook their heads in dismay. They shielded her eyes and slathered her with sunscreen, wishing that she would never see the truth or feel the burn.

They nurtured her into a budding buttercup, flush with joy and beaming with youth. The white petals of the daisy were picked off, one by one, and the world loved her all the more. Her mother painted the walls of the nursery with sunshine, her father spread butter over her pancakes. She spoke her first syllables, and they doted over her, bending to her like feathers bowing to gravity's irresistible tug. In yellow sundresses, she cavorted through the meadows, crowns of dandelions perched atop her glossy hair.

But children do not stay stagnant forever. Her bones grew stronger, her resolve firmer. Her vocal cords swelled, and her tongue grew sharper. She no longer wished to sit still. She yanked fistfuls of her mother's hair, tugged at her father's sleeves.

"We let her be too rambunctious when she was younger," her mother sighed over glasses of wine.

They wanted her to be a peony, soft-skinned and wispy-haired. When she chucked her acrylic paints against the wall, firebrick red rioting against the cabinets, her mother threw up her hands in distress. When she hit a curb and ended up sprawled against the sidewalk, scooter and all, her father decided enough was enough. He set out to buy her tutus, and while she kicked and screamed, her mother wrestled her hair into neat rows of braids. Pastel pink ribbons. French tutors and ballet classes. Be more subdued, they told her. Be less bossy. She thrived at school; a quiet mind eager to learn the ways of the world.

They taught her to be a tulip. To pop with color and stun with vibrance—careful though, to always put others first. To live life with a perennial smile plastered onto her face. She arranged her hair, scrutinized her face in the mirror each day before

leaving the house. Layers of mascara and dollops of concealer. Always orderly, always elegant. Tall and crisp.

"She's a breath of fresh air," they said.

Her irises sparkled, with intelligence, with laughter, with tears. She carried the weight of the world on her shoulders yet managed to float with an angel's aplomb. Dignified, not proud. She learned when to let witty remarks roll off her tongue like raindrops and when to stay silent, stolid even as storm clouds brewed behind her eyes. Learned how to be curious without being nosy. Always say please and thank you.

"What a perfect young lady," they said.

They told her to be a rose. Trimmed and proper. Pulled together, everything swirling about her in perfect unity. Classy and poetic.

"You're old enough to get married now," her grandmother admonished over the phone.

"I want to be a doctor," she'd said. "I don't want to be married yet."

But her father withheld tuition. "Get married first," he said. "Otherwise, you'll end up old and lonely."

And so, she danced and dined, accepted compliments and coffee. Offered gracious smiles and delicate laughs. Spritzes of heavy perfume, dizzying flickers cast by chandeliers. But while suitors offered roses, thorns pricked her, and her silence bled scarlet.

The suitor knelt on the boardwalk before her and presented her with a ring. A diamond, inlaid with platinum, sparkling in the evening light. Passerby's gasped, and she smiled. He was wealthy, suave, intelligent. What more could she want? She held out her left hand. The diamond was all sharp edges, the band was cold. He leaned in to kiss her palm, but the ring slipped off of her downturned finger. She lunged for it, but it was already falling through the cracks in the dock. She collapsed onto the boardwalk, peered into the ocean. Nothing to see except for a swirling black void. Her tears becoming one with the waves, she pulled herself together and picked herself up. Splinters throbbed in her palms. A thousand little stings. Red flushing her cheeks, she ran down the boardwalk, chasing her fiancé who had stormed away.

Lily-of-the-valley. Her mother handed her an ivory bouquet with bell-shaped blossoms.

"You look beautiful," her mother whispered.

She nodded, her thin lips imitating a smile. She turned to the mirror and stepped into her wedding gown. Her shoulders heaved under the weight of lace and tulle. A waterfall of white lies. Layer upon layer, cascading to the floor, drowning her out. A bridesmaid made some stupid joke, and she laughed, peals of laughter freezing in the air like suspended droplets of sea spray. No one could hear her pain.

With the veil covering her eyes she traipsed down the aisle, each footfall shaky and uncertain. Clung to the lilies like her life depended on it. Flower girls flung fistfuls of petals into the air, which descended like ethereal confetti. She tried to tiptoe around them, but the petals were everywhere. By the end of the ceremony, the white petals had turned brown and sickly sweet under the crunch of her heel.

"Was she to blame for
living a life of
fragility? Or was it the
rest of the world, for
pruning her into a pretty
little doll, for indulging
her every need and then
spurning her from the
sacred garden, casting
her down to shame."
~ Steffi Kim

And for all their innocence, the lily-of-the-valley carried a dreadful secret. Pleasant at first sight, but extremely poisonous to consume.

*

But flowers do not, cannot last forever. The silky petals of youth wilted, and her plump skin shriveled, all vivacity leached from her veins. She picked the petals of the daisy, counting them out one by one, and the world loved her not. She gave birth to two daughters, swaddling them up in lilac cocoons. Held them tight against her chest. They were far too light, far too delicate. Too faint of heart, too soft. She would need to teach them soon. The world was a dangerous place.

The knot of marriage grew taught, suffocating her, squeezing out every last breath of freedom. Her husband landed a job across the country. She kissed her mother goodbye, hugged her friends. Felt their fleshy arms wrap around her hollow body, squeezing her when there was nothing left to give.

At her new house, the winds carried an unsettling scent. The grass itched, and the flower buds sneezed pollen. The clouds had a runny nose, splattering the earth in constant drizzles. A March freeze crept over her heart, insidiously biting its way deeper, severing the roots. She was snipped from the vine, wrenched from her support system and transplanted into foreign soil. She wondered if she could ever grow again.

She toiled at work until the sun slipped down the periwinkle sky. Was always trapped in the herd of traffic, always running late to pick up the kids. The candle of love sputtered and waned, conflict rained down and extinguished the last of the flickers. One argument spiraled into a dozen more. When her husband lost his job, he drove home and hurled a plate against the wall. She spent the night kneeling on the hardwood floor, sweeping up the broken pieces of her soul. The toddlers would not stop wailing.

Hindsight was a dangerous game, a gamble between logic and insanity. But her husband was off gambling, so she figured she might as well play the game, teeter the tightrope of sanity. She could not afford to stumble.

If she fell down now, nobody would help her up.

At the tragic age of thirty-eight, she was already past her prime. She yearned to befriend happiness, but Felicity was fickle, Joy was snobby, and Hope passed her by. The train of life was rushing by at alarming speed. Her life was not a sky but a puddle, serving only to reflect her husband's light. There was no way to escape, no alternate path. To hit the brakes, to swerve off the tracks, would be to crash and burn.

*

On a wintry day she sat in the kitchen with the lights off. Fumbled through the mountain of envelopes, wallowing in a glass of wine. But nothing, not even the alcohol itself, could slake her thirst. Her thirst for freedom, for adventure. Her thirst to be young again, exuberant and alive.

In a trance she leaned against the wall, cradling the telephone in her hand. "Mom," she gasped through the line. Her voice broke, a traitorous sob ripping free from her rib cage. "Mom, I can't do it anymore."

"What are you talking about darling?" Her mother's lighthearted voice rang across the line. "No need to be so dramatic."

Hearing her mother's indifference was the piercing blow. A surge of raw emotion, dark and suffocating, welled up inside her, bile rushing up her throat. An unrestrained cry burst free, and she hung up the phone, collapsed onto the floor.

Buried her head in her hands, feeling like a little girl again.

Who was that girl of the past? The girl who threw temper tantrums and screamed with the unbridled roaring of the waves. Who double-crossed fate, thwarted the odds because they were rigged against her. The girl who did as she pleased, refusing to remain silent when the world was unfair.

The girl who would've known what to do.

That girl had never existed.

Not in her lifetime, at least. She had been a fragile daisy, a cloistered buttercup. Deprived of the wind of adventure and the sorrow of the clouds. The peony, so pretty but so helpless. Foreign to thunder, gullible, unprepared for strife. The tulip, manicured to perfection, poised at all costs. Never laughing too loudly, never raising her voice. The rose, liable to its own thorns, eternally doomed by the duplicitous scent of love. And the lily, bound to the valley of domesticity, innocent yet poisonous.

Was she to blame for living a life of fragility? Or was it the rest of the world, for pruning her into a pretty little doll, for indulging her every need and then spurning her from the sacred garden, casting her down to shame. For demanding more of her,

drilling into her, internalizing the mantra that she was not enough. Telling her to mind her manners and not to ask questions. Not to interrupt, not to be abrasive.

*

She knew that the property was foreclosed, that the bank was seizing the house any day now. She knew that it was only a matter of time. The bank accounts had dried up, but she swung by the ATM on her way home from work. Withdrew all she could. It was all going to be taken anyway. Her husband was up to his shoulders in debt.

It was recklessly calculated, what she did that night. She cooked dinner, pretended that all was well. Set a batch of chocolate chip cookies, her husband's favorite, into the oven.

And then, long before the fingers of dawn could reach above the horizon, she woke her daughters. Cradled one in her arms and grasped the other firmly by the hand. With trembling fists, she shifted the car into reverse, backed out of the driveway.

In the deserted house, all was still except for the bleat of her husband's snores. Downstairs, the tantalizing smell of warm chocolate wafted through the kitchen. Soon, the aroma of brown sugar was infused with an undercurrent of smoke.

In all her hurry she had forgotten to turn off the oven.

*

The detectives can't see all that, of course. Naturally, when they stare at her face, all they see is a troubled woman with yellowed teeth and lines of burden etched into her eyes. In her bleak gaze they mistake hopelessness for callousness.

She lacks the words, lacks the conviction to tell her story. Even if she did, the marbles of truth would slip through their clumsy fingers, and they wouldn't understand. Time has stained her, wrinkled her soul. Hung her out to dry like a pilling t-shirt clinging to the clothesline. But she knows that time is potent. She prays that time will bleach her, disintegrate her flaws and make her crisp and pure again. For now, she stays where she is, afraid of the world, afraid of herself.

After a while, even the most patient of therapists give up. They gather their long coats about them, turn on their heel, slam the barred door shut in her face. She doesn't even flinch.

"She wasn't a bad seed," her mother swore to her book club ladies. "I don't know what happened."

But maybe, if she hadn't been forced to be a daisy, a buttercup, a peony, a tulip, a rose. A lily.

Maybe, if she had been endowed with the freedom to be whatever she wanted.

Maybe then, she wouldn't have become poison ivy.

***

Softly
by Phrieda Bogere

I don't feel the need
To act urgently The time
will come And what
happens, happens.

I don't feel the need
To walk with extra layers
In hopes of never getting burned, It won't
sting as bad as I think it will And if it does,
the feeling won't last forever.

I don't feel the need
Of proudly parading the
Ability of having thick skin Endurance
can sometimes be the enemy So it's
nice to finally move softly.

Thorn & Bloom

a literary
magazine

Thank you to everyone who submitted their work and entrusted us with their words—we are honoured to hold space for your voices.

A special heartfelt thank you to Shikha S. Lamba, a true muse and one of our greatest supporters. Your unwavering presence, especially in moments of doubt and struggle, means more than words can express.

CONTACT INFO:

www.redrosethorns.com
/
contact@redrosethorns.com
/
@redrosethorns